Designed by Flowerpot Press in Franklin, TN.
www.FlowerpotPress.com
Designer: Stephanie Meyers
Editor: Katrine Crow
ROR-0808-0106
ISBN: 978-1-4867-1260-1
Made in China/Fabriqué en Chine

The Owl and the Kitty Cat

Melissa Everett

Illustrated by Mark Kummer

The Owl and the Kitty Cat
went to sea,
In a bright green sailing boat.

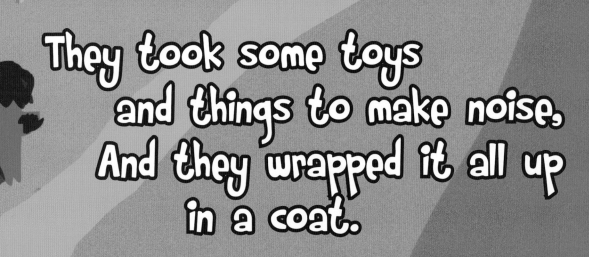

They took some toys
and things to make noise,
And they wrapped it all up
in a coat.

The Owl stared up to the stars in the sky,
And started to play his guitar...

"O, lovely Kitty! O, Kitty! O, my!
What a beautiful Kitty you are,
you are, you are,
What a beautiful
Kitty you are!"

Kitty said to the Owl,
"You elegant Fowl,
I love it whenever you sing.
My husband to be,
will you please marry me?"

He said, "But, I haven't a ring."

They sailed away
For a year and a day,
To the land where
the Doodle-Tree grows...

And there, in a wood,
a giant bull stood,
With a ring
at the end of his nose,
his nose,
his nose,
With a ring at the end of his nose.

"Big Bull, if I holler
will you sell for a dollar,
Your ring?" Said the Bull, "Yes I will."
So they took it away,
and were married next day,
By the Kangaroo up on the hill.

And hand in hand
on the edge of
the sand,
They danced
by the light
of the moon,

the moon,
the moon,
They danced
by the light
of the moon.